Stone Age Tales

The Great Monster

D0413096

BLOOMSBURY EDUCATION
Bloomsbury Publishing Plc
50 Bedford Square, London, WC1B 3DP, UK

BLOOMSBURY, BLOOMSBURY EDUCATION and
the Diana logo are trademarks of Bloomsbury Publishing Plc

First published in Great Britain in 2018 by Bloomsbury Publishing Plc

ISBN: PB: 978 1 4729 5035 2; ePub: 978 1 4729 5036 9; ePDF: 978 1 4729 5034 5

2 4 6 8 10 9 7 5 3 1

Text design by Amy Cooper Design

Printed and bound in the UK by CPI Group (UK) Ltd, Croydon CR0 4YY

To find out more about our authors and books visit www.bloomsbury.com
and sign up for our newsletters

TERRY DEARY

Stone Age Tales

The Great Monster

Illustrated by
Tambe

BLOOMSBURY EDUCATION
AN IMPRINT OF BLOOMSBURY

LONDON OXFORD NEW YORK NEW DELHI SYDNEY

Contents

1

The Baby and the Eagle

Mesopotamia, 2,500 years ago

Sin-leqi was small and his arms were like twigs.

'You're too weak to hunt,' his brothers said. 'Stay at home and fetch water... if you can carry the buckets,' they laughed.

Sin-leqi smiled and said, 'Hunt the bulls by the river and bring me meat.'

'What will you give us in return?' the oldest brother asked, as he strapped on his sandals.

'I will give you a story,' Sin-leqi promised.

'Make sure the water tanks are filled

first,' his uncle said, picking up his bow, his spear and his arrows.

'Of course,' Sin-leqi promised. The hunters set off on the hot and dusty road to the valley to see if they could catch cattle drinking from the river. It was dangerous work.

Sometimes the herds of cows would be guarded by a massive bull; sometimes a mountain lion prowled and the hunters were hunted by the fangs and claws and jaws of a beast as fast as the summer wind.

Sin-leqi watched them go. He walked to the temple and the priest gave him some clay tablets to read. 'One day *you* will be the priest, Sin-leqi.'

After a day reading in the cool courtyard, the boy remembered he was supposed to fill the family water tanks. The hunters would be home soon.

He picked up two buckets and placed them on the roadway where the mud-brick houses stood. 'Who wants a story?' he called. Five smaller children ran from the houses, shouting, 'Me, Sin-leqi – me, me, me.'

Sin-leqi's dark eyes sparkled in the dusty sun and he held a mud tablet in his small hands. 'It will take me time to read the old story,' he sighed. 'And, of course, I have to fill our water tank before my family returns from hunting.'

One of the children, a girl, Ninsun, was the same age as Sin-leqi and just as wise. 'I know what you want us to say. You want us to say that *we* will fill your water tanks while you sit in the shade and read the old stories. Then, when we've done your work for you, you will give us a story?'

The boy spread his thin hands. 'Well, I *could* carry my own water, but then you'd have to wait until sunset for the story.'

'No-o,' the other children groaned.

'Come on,' Ninsun sighed. 'Let's do his work.' She turned and stared at Sin-leqi. 'But it had better be a good story.'

And, when the scorching sun was setting, low in the sky, the hunters came home. They sat alongside the children in the feasting hall and Sin-leqi told a story that was thousands of years old.

*

Now the king of Babylon, Suchorus, was as cruel as fire. One day, in his capital city of Uruk, a wise woman came to him and told him she could see into the future.

'What will happen to me?' Suchorus asked.

'You will be killed and the killer will take your throne,' the wise woman said.

And Suchorus was afraid. 'Who will kill me?' he asked.

'Your own grandson, Gilgamesh, will kill you,' she replied.

Suchorus stroked his long, dark beard. 'Gilgamesh? He is a baby. If I kill him now, he won't grow up to kill me.'

'You cannot cheat the future. The gods have said Gilgamesh will live to rule this land.'

'Curse the gods,' the cruel king cried. He rose from his throne and pushed past the wise woman. He climbed the steps to a small room in the high tower. A nurse was feeding the baby, Gilgamesh.

Suchorus snatched the babe from the woman and walked over to the high window in the high tower. He pushed open the shutters that were keeping the room cool from the harsh sun.

Then Suchorus reached out and held the baby out of the window. The nurse screamed.

(The children listening to Sin-leqi's story screamed, and stretched their eyes, too.)

And Suchorus opened his hands and let the baby Gilgamesh fall. He tumbled and turned like a straw in the wind towards the hard yard below.

But a hunting eagle was flying past the palace when it saw the baby fall. It closed its wings and dropped towards the child, and its mighty claws caught Gilgamesh and snatched him up before the baby hit the ground.

It soared away and then landed in a palace garden to lay the baby down and tear its flesh for dinner. But the king's old gardener saw it, and raised his spade and rushed towards the eagle. The bird gave a cry of rage and flew away, and left the baby lying there.

The gardener told the baby's mother that the child was safe inside his humble hut – but the mother knew Suchorus would try and try again, until her babe was dead.

So, she took the child and placed it in a basket, and she covered the basket in tar and set it loose upon the waters of the great river. It was washed to safety and found by a woman washing clothes beside the river shore.

That good woman raised Gilgamesh as her own child. He grew up to be a strong warrior, the strongest in all of Uruk. He marched to the city and told the people he was king. Suchorus left the palace and rushed at Gilgamesh with his sword.

The two mighty men fought all day

without rest. But, as evening stars were rising in the sky, the sword of Suchorus broke and Gilgamesh slew him.

And so, the wise one's story came to pass. The people of the city cheered their new king. They cheered too soon. Suchorus had been cruel – but Gilgamesh would be crueller still.

*

Sin-leqi finished his story and the children clapped. Ninsun said, 'And what happened next?'

'Yes, what happened next?' the hunters cried.

Sin-leqi gave a shrug. 'I'll tell what happened next when you return from your hunting tomorrow evening. I need to read the next tablet in the temple tomorrow. Then I can tell the tale of Enkidu.'

'I want to hear it now,' Ninsun demanded.

Sin-leqi grinned. 'You'll have to wait.'

The girl ground her teeth. 'They said Gilgamesh was cruel. But you are worse.' She stamped her feet and went off home.

2

The King and the Monster

When Sin-leqi's brothers returned from the hunt the next evening, they were dragging a dead bull by the horns. They took it to the feasting hall in the middle of the city and crowds gathered around.

Their uncle began to carve it. First he gave a slice of the best rump to the priest. The priest would take it to the temple, cook it and lay it on the altar to say thank you to the gods.

Ninsun snorted, 'When the gods don't eat it, then the fat priest will eat it all himself.'

'Hush, girl,' her mother said.

'You know it's true,' Ninsun muttered.

Sin-leqi's family then traded pieces of the beef with the people of the town – beef for new arrows, beef for wine, beef for bread and beef for new wool tunics.

Then it was time to have their own feast. As they began to share it, the oldest brother said, 'Of course, Sin-leqi can't have any beef until he has told us a story.'

The family laughed, as if it were a joke. But Sin-leqi knew he wouldn't get a singed scrap until he had told a tale.

Ninsun crept through the open door and hid in the shadows behind the feasting family to listen. Sin-leqi began.

*

Suchorus, the king of Uruk, had been cruel to some of the people. Gilgamesh would be crueller still. Oh, but Gilgamesh was cruel to *all* of the people.

The women were made to dance for him. The men were made to work, building him a fine palace, temple towers and high walls around Uruk, and looking after his orchards and fields.

Most days, the young warriors had to fight one another so Gilgamesh could watch the sport. At the end of the contests, Gilgamesh would fight the winner. Every time, Gilgamesh would win.

'Weaklings and sheep,' he sneered. 'You are not fit to serve a great king like me.'

The people grew tired of the bully-king and learned to hate him. Yet no one had the power to stand up against him. So, one of the toothless old women told them what to do. 'Ask the gods for help,' she said.

'It's so simple – why didn't I think of that?' a small man said.

'Well, I *did* think of it,' his wife said, 'but I didn't want to make you look stupid by saying it before you did.'

On a moonless night, a group of people crept through the silent streets of Uruk. There was one person from every family, and the old, wise woman carried a roasted duck as a gift to the gods.

They came to the huge temple gates – the gates that it had taken an army of the king's workers a river of sweat to build.

The priest opened the gates and let the people in. 'Welcome, my people,' the priest said.

'Shhhh,' the people said.

'Don't you tell me to shush in my own temple. You can all get out if you're going to be like that.' He began to close the mighty gate. 'Go on, get out.'

'We've brought the gods a tasty roast duck,' a woman said.

'Come in,' the priest said. 'I'd better taste the leg of that bird to make sure it's fit for the gods,' he said, and he chewed on it as the fat dribbled down his chin. 'Now, what can I do for you?'

And the people of Uruk told him – and he passed on their message to the gods, and the gods heard the Uruk people's prayers.

The next day, when Gilgamesh had fought and beaten the champion of the city, he jeered, 'Weaklings and sheep. You are not fit to serve a great king like me.'

'No,' said the old wise woman. 'But maybe there is one on the hill outside Uruk who could defeat you.'

'No man can defeat me,' Gilgamesh roared.

'Who says it's a man? It *could* be a woman,' the old, wise woman muttered through her gums.

'It's a woman?' Gilgamesh gasped.

'No, it's a man... I was just saying it could have been a woman.'

Gilgamesh sighed. He hated people who made clever remarks like that. 'So, who *is* this man?'

'His name is Enkidu,' the priest piped up. 'He is a wild man sent from the goddess Aruru to teach you a lesson.'

'Good,' the king crowed. 'I shall defeat him and show I am greater than the gods. How will I know this man when I meet him?'

The priest gave a chuckle. 'Well, Your Majesty, he is covered from head to toe in hair. He is a hairy monster.'

'He will be a *dead* hairy monster when I've finished with him,' Gilgamesh promised.

'My dad's dead hairy,' a little boy said.

The king marched out of Uruk to the hill by the river. Enkidu waited for him, quiet as the stones.

Gilgamesh roared at him, 'I am Gilgamesh, ruler of the greatest empire the world has ever seen, slayer of King Suchorus, unbeaten in five hundred fights with the champions of Uruk. Now I shall defeat the hairy champion of the gods. I shall cut off your head, Enkidu, slice your flesh and feed it to my hunting dogs, I shall boil your bones and... What? What's the matter?'

'Sorry, Gil – I was just yawning. When are you going to finish flapping your tongue and start fighting?'

The king was enraged and rushed at the monster. Their swords clashed with a clang that rang out on Cedar Mountain, miles away.

The people had followed their king and started to cheer. But, as the sun crawled across the heavens, their cheering grew weak – for the fight looked like it would never end. The fighters stood toe to toe, and swung and swiped with swords. By nightfall, the people had gone home to bed.

No one slept because the singing swords went on all night. Next morning, a few weary people went to watch more of the fight. At last, Enkidu's sword cut Gilgamesh, who stepped back. The hairy monster leapt forward to finish the king. He raised his sword high... and then his

foot skidded in the blood of Gilgamesh, and he landed with a crunch that shook the ground. The king was up and had his sword at the throat of Enkidu. Gilgamesh roared.

'Stop,' the priest cried. 'You have to stop, Your Majesty.'

'Why?'

And the priest told him.

*

'Why?' the hunters said, like an echo.

Sin-leqi spread his hands. 'I read the story from some old tablets they keep in the temple. It's a slow job. I will read more tomorrow.'

'And will you tell us what happened to Gilgamesh and Enkidu?'

Sin-leqi shrugged. 'I can't do that if you force me to go out hunting with you, brothers.'

'No,' the old uncle said. 'You stay at the temple. Read the tablets. We'll hunt for meat and feed you when we return.'

Sin-leqi sighed. 'It doesn't seem fair. Are you sure?'

'We're sure.'

In the shadows of the corner, the girl Ninsun was the only one who saw a small smile creep over Sin-leqi's face – a smile that said he had done something clever.

3

The Axe and the Armour

The next evening, Sin-leqi walked from the temple to the feasting hall, where a fine ox was roasting. The girl Ninsun ran after him. 'You know the story of Gilgamesh, don't you?' she hissed.

'I read some more of it today,' Sin-leqi said.

'No, I mean you know the whole story,' the girl said. 'Last night you stopped at an exciting part so the hunters would have to hear more tonight... and feed you again. You feast well but you do no work.'

Sin-leqi stopped and glared at her. 'Storytelling is work,' he said.

'Not like building walls or making spears or cutting down trees,' she argued.

'No,' he said with a sigh.

'And not even as hard as the women's work I'm learning: washing clothes and fetching water and making clothes.'

'Maybe not.'

Suddenly Ninsun stopped and clutched at Sin-leqi's sleeve. 'Teach me to read. We can learn twice as many stories if we work together.'

Sin-leqi laughed. 'Work together? I thought storytelling wasn't work, you said.'

The girl slapped his arm. 'You know what

I mean. I don't want to sweat by the river in the noonday sun, washing clothes. I want to sit in the cool temple, with you, reading stories and telling them at the fireside each night.'

Sin-leqi gave a sharp nod. 'Let's see if the story works tonight.' They walked together into the hall. The boy ate well, and then went on with the story.

*

The priest from the temple at Uruk cried, 'Listen, Gilgamesh.'

The king stopped his sword a hair's width from the throat of the wild man, Enkidu.

The priest panted, 'I was in the temple when a great wind sprang up and howled through the pillars. And in the howling, I heard the voice of the goddess Ishtar. She sent a message to you, Gilgamesh.'

'Yes, the gods speak to me,' the king said.

'I am almost a god myself.' The king stroked his long, black hair and patted his thick beard. 'I am handsome enough to be a god,' he told the people of Uruk.

'I've got a swine in my fields that's better looking than him,' an old woman muttered. She didn't mutter very loudly.

'What was the message from Ishtar?'

'She wants you to go to Cedar Mountain, to cut down a great holy cedar tree,' the priest said, 'and use the wood to build a gate for Uruk.'

'No one is allowed to cut down the cedars,' a woman wailed.

'Yes, I was about to say that,' Gilgamesh grumped.

'The demon Humbaba guards it,' the woman went on.

'Yes, I know that too. Stop telling me things I already know.'

'You don't know if you can defeat the demon,' the woman said.

'You are wrong. I *do* know I *can't* defeat a demon. Is the goddess Ishtar trying to get me killed?'

'I hope so,' the old woman whispered.

Then the wild man on the ground spoke. 'I was born wild and brought up by the forest animals,' he said. 'Shepherds in the hills tamed me and taught me to be human. All things happen for a reason.'

35

'And what's the reason you learned to be human?' Gilgamesh asked.

'To help you kill Humbaba, Your Kingship. A demon can fight a man like you, or a beast like me – but together we might defeat him.'

Gilgamesh nodded, and the thick ringlets under his crown waved in the breeze that rolled down from the hills.

He stretched out a hand and grasped Enkidu's hairy hand. 'You are right, my friend.'

'Your friend?' the monster said.

Gilgamesh looked suddenly shy. 'I would like you to be my friend,' he said. 'I am a great man. You are a great monster. Think of the adventures we could have together.'

'We could start with cutting down the holy cedar tree for the goddess Ishtar,' Enkidu said, as he brushed the dusty soil off his back where he had slipped and fallen to the ground.

The dust rose in a cloud and made the watching old woman sneeze. 'You need a good bath before you go, if you ask me,' she sniffled.

Enkidu was taken back to the palace and bathed in the milk of twenty asses. Then he was fed with the richest food in the land, from the tongues of a thousand larks to the brains of a butchered bear.

When he had feasted and rested for a week, the king's servants made him armour of the hardest boiled leather, and gave him a spear, a shield and a sword.

But Enkidu said he wanted an axe with a long handle, so that is what they made him. The axe was so heavy it took two strong men to lift it. Enkidu lifted it with one hand.

'This will cut down a cedar tree with one blow,' he boasted.

'One blow?' His new friend Gilgamesh gasped.

'Well... maybe two,' Enkidu said.

The palace kitchens filled sacks with beef and ox tongues – they had run out of larks – and with bread and fruits. The two warriors carried leather bottles of water and wine.

No one in Uruk worked that day. They all went to the old and rotten wooden gates to say goodbye to the heroes.

'Goodbye,' an old man cried. 'Come home safe.'

'Good riddance,' the old woman snapped, sourly. 'I don't care if you never come back at all.'

'We need new gates,' the old man reminded her.

The old woman took a deep breath. 'Come home safe,' she called.

And so, Gilgamesh and Enkidu set off. They climbed hills and snow-capped mountains. They hacked through forests and fought off the wild creatures that lived there.

And on the seventh day, they reached the far side of the trees and looked out at the gloomy, looming Cedar Mountain.

'What happened next, Sin-leqi?' the hunters asked.

'Did they slay the demon Humbaba?'

The boy shrugged. 'I'll tell you tomorrow, when I've read the next tablet.'

'Awwww,' the hunters groaned.

In the shadows of the hall wall, the girl Ninsun laughed softly. 'Clever boy, Sin-leqi. Very clever.'

4
The Demon and the Cedar

Ninsun was a quick learner, and Sin-leqi found it was good to share the stories on the old clay tablets. 'But who taught *you* to read?' the girl asked.

'The priest in the temple,' he replied. 'He thinks I may take his job one day.'

'You want to be a priest?' Ninsun asked.

'It's better than hunting... I like eating meat, but I hate the killing and the skinning and the blood.'

'I like eating meat too,' Ninsun said. 'You could give me some of yours tonight when your brothers feast.'

'I only have enough for myself,' he said with a scowl.

'Ask for more,' the girl said. Sin-leqi was about to argue, but she went on, 'I am going to help you. You are helping me to read, so I will help you to tell a better story.'

'You think I need help?'

'Yes – the first part of the story ends tonight. Then your brothers will make you hunt, kill and get blood all over your hands. I can tell you how to leave them wanting to hear more tomorrow night... and the night after.'

'Can you?' Sin-leqi said.

'Come on. Let's get to the feasting hall. All that reading's made me hungry.'

And so they hurried through the cool evening dust on the street. Sin-leqi told his tale...

*

The heroes heard the demon Humbaba roar before they saw him. The mountain shook and rocks tumbled towards them, but the two warriors were too quick.

Humbaba sent a wild bull, but Gilgamesh killed it with his sword. A thunderbird appeared, breathing fire, but Gilgamesh threw his spear into its heart.

At last, the demon stood before them – a human shape, but with seven layers of armour. His sword was as long as a man is tall, and his breath was foul enough to melt the mountain snows.

'I am Gilgamesh,' the king said. 'I have

45

come to take the greatest cedar in the forest, to build new gates for Uruk.'

'Is that what you think, little man?' the demon boomed. 'I will kill you. I will cut open your belly and feed your flesh to the birds.'

'Maybe we will kill you first,' Enkidu said.

'Hah,' the demon sneered. 'I am not afraid of a hairy man who looks like a dog. When I've killed Gilgamesh, I shall kill you and feed you to the fishes in the river.

He raised his huge sword and whirled it round his head. Gilgamesh stepped back, afraid. But Enkidu said, 'Forward, my friend – don't be afraid.'

Gilgamesh was trembling. 'I am not afraid... I am just being careful.'

'Then *carefully* aim your spear at Humbaba's heart,' Enkidu told the king.

The spear flew fast and true. It tore through the first coat of armour, it ripped into the second and it went clear through the third. The spear made a hole in the fourth layer, but slowed down and hardly scratched the fifth, where it stopped.

Humbaba snapped the mighty spear shaft like a twig. He threw it aside, lifted his sword again and brought it down on Gilgamesh.

The king tried to meet the blow with his own sword, but it shattered in his hand. Gilgamesh tumbled back and the demon's sword buried itself in the rocky ground. Enkidu swung his axe and, before Humbaba could free his sword, the hairy man had hacked at the demon's arm. That arm was thick as a cedar tree and, though it bled, the blow didn't stop Humbaba pulling his sword from the earth and marching forward to finish Gilgamesh. 'It's a scratch, hairy man, a scratch. You can watch as I slice your king open...'

'You cannot kill us,' Enkidu cried.

The demon blinked. 'I think you will find that spilling your king's guts on the ground *will* kill him, little man.'

'The god Shamash will save us,'

Gilgamesh shouted, struggling to his feet.

'I can't see him,' Humbaba said, and laughed.

But, as he laughed, the skies turned black and the wind began to swirl and raise the dust. Shamash sent thirteen winds, and each one threw dust in the demon's eyes.

Humbaba cried out and dropped his sword to rub his eyes, and stumbled towards the river. When he felt the icy river at his feet, he knelt and scooped the water to wash out the dust.

Humbaba shook his head and looked up. Gilgamesh was holding the demon's mighty sword.

'Spare me,' Humbaba wailed. He looked at the king, with tears washing the last of the dust from his eyes. 'Spare me, the way you once spared Enkidu.'

The king turned to the hairy man. 'If I let

him live, he may serve us. He could guard Uruk better than cedar gates.'

The demon gave an ugly twist of the face that was meant to be a smile. 'Dear Gilgamesh, you can be king of the forest. I will cut the trees for you, and be your slave.'

Enkidu shook his head. 'Never trust a demon, my dear friend. He is lying. Kill him.' And, with a fierce blow, Gilgamesh struck the head off the demon.

The heroes entered the forest and cut down the greatest cedar, and then a smaller one.

They built a raft from the smaller tree and returned home down the river with the giant tree... and the head of Humbaba.

And so, the heroes' first adventure ended.

The hunters clapped loudly. 'A good story, Sin-leqi,' his uncle said. 'Tomorrow you can be Gilgamesh and slay a monster bull for us to eat. That would be fun to watch.' The hunters laughed.

'No,' came a voice from the shadows. Ninsun stepped forward. 'If you make Sin-leqi hunt, you will never hear the other adventures of Gilgamesh.'

'What other adventures?' a hunter asked.

'You won't hear about the goddess who fell in love with Gilgamesh, and what terrible punishment followed when he turned her down. You won't hear about the king's search for the secret of life. There are lots of stories.'

'How do you know?' Sin-leqi's uncle asked. 'You can't read. Girls can't read.'

Ninsun gave him her warmest smile. 'But I can.'

'It's all wrong, girls reading,' a hunter grumbled.

'Ah, but I am going to be a priestess,' Ninsun told him.

'Are you?' the man asked.

'Are you?' Sin-leqi asked.

'Yes. If you can be a priest in the temple, Sin-leqi, then I can be a priestess. There are lots of goddesses and they need a woman to look after them.'

Sin-leqi nodded wisely. 'I suppose the goddesses will need lots of gifts of food.'

'Mmmm,' the girl agreed. 'Now let's go,' she said, and took Sin-leqi by the hand.

'Where are we going?' the boy asked, as she pulled him down the street.

'To the temple, of course. You are going to tell the priest that the temple needs me as a priestess.'

'Why am I going to do that?'

Ninsun stopped, and peered at the boy in the gloom. 'Because we are friends... like Gilgamesh and Enkidu. I just saved you from the hunt the way Enkidu saved Gilgamesh from Humbaba. See?'

Sin-leqi grinned. 'So, I am Gilgamesh the handsome and strong. That makes you

Enkidu, the ugly one. You'll be good at that.'

Ninsun gave a cry of rage, but wise Sin-leqi was already running away from her. He didn't stop until they reached the temple – their new home.

FACT FILE

The Story

The legend of Gilgamesh is a myth – an old story. People in the Stone Age must have told lots of stories. We can guess the stories must have been about heroes and gods and monsters.

Then, 5,200 years ago, the Sumerian people of Mesopotamia (the place that is now Iraq) invented writing. The story of Gilgamesh is probably the earliest story that we know was written down. It was written about 4,000 years ago, and parts of the story were copied around 3,000 years ago. It is this copy that tells most of the ancient story.

The True Story

Some historians believe that the story of Gilgamesh was not just a fairy-tale. They say that there really was a King Gilgamesh, and that he was cruel to his people until one man, Enkidu, stood up to the bully-king. They became friends and Gilgamesh learned to be a kinder man.

Sin-leqi-unninni

Sin-leqi-unninni was a priest who lived in Mesopotamia around 3,000 years ago. He made copies of the old stories. King Ashurbanipal had a copy of Sin-leqi's stories in his library. They were forgotten for 1,500 years, but then found in the ruins of the king's palace around 600 BCE.

Sin-leqi-unninni's name means 'the moon god hears my prayers'.

YOU TRY

Monster Mash-up

People have been making up monsters and strange beasts for a long time. They appear in cave-paintings and are still popular in films and books today.

Some of the most famous are:

Dragons: Fire-breathing lizards with scaly skin, serpent eyes, bat wings and talons.

Griffins: Creatures that guard the gods. A griffin had the body, tail and back legs of a lion, the head and wings of an eagle, and an eagle's talons for front feet.

Egyptian gods: Humans with animal heads, like jackal-headed Anubis, cobra-headed Amunet, lion-headed Sekhmet and falcon-headed Horus.

Kamadhenu: The mother of all cattle in India. She was a cow with a human head, a peacock tail and bird wings.

Can you draw and name a completely new monster, made up of bits of other animals and humans?

The Story Goes On...

You have read the story of Gilgamesh and how Humbaba was killed. The next tablet of Sin-leqi goes on with the story.

• The goddess Ishtar, the goddess of love and war, wants to marry Gilgamesh.

• Gilgamesh refuses, so Ishtar sends the 'Bull of Heaven' to punish the people of Uruk with drought, famine and plague.

• Gilgamesh and Enkidu slay the beast, and throw the bull's back legs in the face of Ishtar.

• Ishtar sends a nasty disease to kill Enkidu.

Can you write this story as if you are Sin-leqi?

Quaint Cure

Enkidu died of the terrible disease sent by Ishtar, slowly and in great pain. Can you invent a medicine to save him? Make a list of the things you will use BUT they must all begin with the letter 'M'!

Terry Deary's Stone Age Tales

ISBN: 978 1 4729 5026 0

ISBN: 978 1 4729 5031 4

ISBN: 978 1 4729 5035 2

ISBN: 978 1 4729 5040 6

Look out for more exciting
stories set in the Stone Age!